THE GRUNT AND THE GROUCH

Big Splash!

STONE ARCH BOOKS

a capstone imprint

First published in the United States in 2012
by Stone Arch Books
A Capstone Imprint
1710 Roe Crest Drive
North Mankato, Minnesota 56003
www.capstonepub.com

First published by
Stripes Publishing
1 The Coda Centre, 189 Munster Road
London SW6 6AW

Text © Tracey Corderoy 2010
Cover Illustrations © Lee Wildish 2010
Interior Illustrations © Artful Doodlers

Library of Congress Cataloging-in-Publication Data is available on
the Library of Congress website.

ISBN: 978-1-4342-4602-8 (hardcover)
ISBN: 978-1-4342-4268-6 (paperback)

Summary: The Grunt and the Grouch crash the opening of the
local pool, get tangled up on a camping trip, and babysit Grunt's
trouble-making cousin.

Printed in the United States of America in Stevens Point, Wisconsin.
042012   006678WZF12

THE GRUNT AND THE GROUCH

Big Splash!

Written by
TRACEY CORDEROY

Illustrated by
LEE WILDISH

CONTENTS

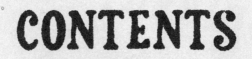

Chapter 1

SQUEEEEEZE! The Grunt wriggled into his jacket and tried to button it across his stomach. It felt very small and very tight.

"Grouchy!" he said. "Did you accidentally take my jacket?"

"Nope!" The Grouch said with a laugh. "But yours looks like it shrunk!"

"That's impossible!" The Grunt yelled. "I've never washed it!"

He plopped himself down in his

favorite chair. But something was
wrong.

"Arrggh!" he yelled. "I'm stuck!"

The Grunt wiggled around, but he
was wedged into the chair.

"What's going on?" he yelled.

Grouchy poked Grunty's tummy.

"You're bigger than you used to be!" The

Grouch said. "You need to eat healthy food and start exercising — maybe then your jacket will fit again!"

The Grouch pulled Grunty out of the chair. "Come on!" he cried. "Let's play ping pong! That's great exercise."

Grunty groaned. "Okay," he muttered. "If I have to."

Grouchy raced into the kitchen with Grunty thumping behind.

"What should we use for paddles?" The Grouch asked. He hurried to the sink, piled high with dirty dishes, and pulled out two filthy pans. "There!" he exclaimed. "These are perfect!"

Next, Grouchy searched through the cupboards and the fridge for something to use as a ping-pong ball. Soon he spotted just the thing.

"Aha!" he exclaimed, clapping his hands. "Eggs!"

Grouchy grabbed the carton of eggs, placed it on the kitchen table, and

opened the lid. "You serve first!" he cried.

The big purple troll tossed an egg into the air and whacked it with his paddle.

SPLAT! The egg exploded all over his head!

IT'S RAINING EGGS! TROLLIFIC!

Grunty stuck out his tongue as egg dripped down his face. "Mmmm," he said as he slurped. "These ping-pong balls are delicious!"

"My turn!" cried Grouchy. He grabbed three eggs and threw them in the air, smashing each one with his pan.

The trolls kept playing, but before they knew it, they'd run out of balls.

"Now what?" grumbled Grunty. He flopped down at the table, grabbed the newspaper, and started searching for other exercise ideas.

"A fun run — yuck!" he grunted. "Knit yourself fit? No thanks!" After a while, he looked up. "Grouchy, what are you doing?"

Grouchy's face was covered with icing. "I'm just having a hairy cake."

"But those are to share!" cried Grunty. "Gimme one!"

"No way!" Grouchy replied. "You're eating healthy stuff now, remember?"

He yanked a hair off his cake and handed it to Grunty. "This should be okay, but just one!"

Grunty scowled and tossed the hair away. He was about to fling the newspaper after it when something caught his eye.

"Look!" he cried, waving the paper at Grouchy. "There's a new swimming pool in town. Splash Tropicana!"

"Oooh!" Grouchy said. "It has slides and everything! And swimming would help you get in shape! Can we go? Please, please, Grunty, can we?"

Grunty read the ad again. The pool
was opening that very afternoon. And
for one day only, it was free!

The Grunt grinned. "Time to fish out
our swimming trunks!" he exclaimed.
He leaped to his feet and thundered
upstairs.

"And my rubber floatie!" Grouchy added, hurrying after him. "But wait . . . what if the water makes us clean?"

"Don't worry!" Grunty cried. "We can roll in some mud on the way home!"

Chapter 2

Five minutes later, the trolls were
ready to go. Grunty decided that they
should jog to the pool since they were
being healthy. But they'd only made it to
the end of the road when . . .

"Wait . . ." Grunty puffed. "Bus! Jump
on!"

The two trolls clambered onboard,
and Grunty collapsed into a seat.

"You can't be tired already!" The Grouch said.

"I'm not," Grunty said, letting out a loud yawn. "See, I'm wide awake!"

With that, he closed his eyes and fell asleep. He spent the rest of the journey snoring noisily while Grouchy jogged in place in the aisle.

Finally, the bus pulled up in front of a large building.

"Grunty! Wake up!" Grouchy cried. "We're here! We're at Splash Tropicana!"

The trolls hurried off the bus and raced to the main door. A man and his son were just about to go inside.

"Hurry up!" cried Grunty, trying to push past them.

"No pushing, please!" the man said.

He opened the door, and his son walked in with the trolls hot on his heels. "No manners!" the man grumbled.

Grunt and Grouch found themselves standing in a bright lobby with surfboards hanging on the walls and palm trees growing in pots.

The man stopped to look at a poster

Splash Tropicona
RULES

NO RUNNING.
NO PUSHING.
NO DUNKING.
NO SHOUTING.
NO DIVE-BOMBING.
NO SPLASHING.

before heading off to the changing room. The trolls groaned. It was a poster of rules.

"No pushing!" Grunty said. "No shouting, no splashing! What *can* we do?"

"It doesn't say 'no burping'," Grouchy whispered. So the trolls let out two gigantic burps, and then raced away to get changed!

The locker room was sparkling white and packed with excited people. The trolls looked around eagerly, but all the stalls were full.

Suddenly, two doors clicked open and the father and son from the lobby walked out wearing matching brown bathing suits.

"All set!" the boy said, handing his
dad a stack of neatly folded clothes.

His dad smiled. "Good job, Michael!"

"Look!" cried Grunty. "Two empty
stalls. Quick!"

But as they raced across the wet floor,

Grunty slipped. "Arrgh!" he cried, flying through the air. "HELP!"

He landed with a loud thud and skidded into the man, knocking the clothes he was holding onto the floor.

"Whoops!" cried Grouchy. He picked the clothes up and tossed them back to the man in a messy pile.

The man scowled at the trolls. "Follow me, Michael," he said to his son. "And stay away from those two in the pool!"

He placed their clothes in a locker and headed for the showers. Just then, the trolls burst out of their changing rooms.

"Let's go!" Grunty yelled.

The Grunt and The Grouch zipped

across the locker room and dumped
their clothes in a locker.

"Forget the showers!" Grunty said.
"Let's get to the pool! There's plenty of
water there we can wash off in!"

They hurried through the locker
room door to find the pool packed with

kids. Some were whizzing down brightly colored slides while others swam in the water.

"Wow!" gasped Grunty. "Race you to the diving boards!"

The trolls sprinted off, but they hadn't gone far when they heard a loud whistle. A lifeguard sitting on a tall chair held up a NO RUNNING! sign.

"Oops!" Grouchy said. "We forgot!"

The trolls waddled off as fast as they could.

"Let's go up to the very top diving board!" said Grunty.

Chapter 3

The trolls climbed up to the highest diving board and began to bounce into the air.

"Yippee!" they yelled. "We're flying!"

"Dad!" one of the kids yelled. "Look! Up there!"

Everyone in the pool gazed up, open-mouthed, as the trolls came crashing down toward the water.

"Wheeeeee!" cried Grunty. He held his nose as he hit the water with a huge . . .

SPLASH!

The force of Grunty's cannonball sent everyone shooting out of the water and onto the side of the pool in a soggy tangle.

"This is outrageous!" someone yelled. "Lifeguard! They're breaking the rules!"

The lifeguard tried to blow his whistle, but it was filled with water. Instead, he thrust a "NO CANNONBALLS!" sign into the air.

"Sorry!" Grouchy called. "We couldn't

help it. It was Grunty's big fat tummy
that did it!"

The trolls started playing in the pool
as kids nervously made their way back
into the water.

After a while, the water began to
wash the trolls clean, and soon the pool

was filled with disgusting objects. Flies,
fleas, spiders, and worms, as well as
three squashed pickles and a chunk of
moldy cheese, floated near the trolls.

They grabbed what they could and
stuffed them into their trunks, but most
of their goodies went floating away.

"Never mind!" said Grouchy. "Let's go
down the slide. Come on!"

The trolls hurried out of the pool and up the steps leading to the waterslide. "This is gonna be trollrific!" Grouchy said excitedly.

The slide was long and twisty and made from see-through yellow plastic. It looked like a giant toilet-paper roll.

"Me first!" Grunty said when they reached the top of the stairs. "Here I gooooooo!"

Grunty shot off down the slide, with Grouchy zooming behind. Down they went, faster and faster. They could see a bend approaching. Then suddenly . . . *THUNK!*

"I'm stuck!" Grunty yelled, jiggling around. "I can't fit around the bend!"

"Look ouuutt!" cried Grouchy. He

whizzed down and crashed straight into
Grunty. Ooof!

"Oh, no!" Grouchy yelled, looking
behind him. "Someone's coming!"

The father and son they'd seen in the
locker room careened around the bend

and crashed into Grouchy. "OW!" they yelled.

"Move!" the man yelled.

"I can't!" said Grouchy. "Grunty's stuck!"

The Grunt tried to wriggle free, but it was no use.

"Let the air out of his floaties!" the boy suggested.

"Good idea!" his father replied. He leaned forward and yanked the plugs out of the floaties on Grunty's arms. The air hissed out noisily and — *WHOOSH!* — away they all went!

The group hurtled out of the end of the slide and landed in the water with an enormous plop!

"Hey!" one of the lifeguards yelled

through a megaphone. "You two trolls, out! NOW!"

Grunty and Grouchy sighed and climbed out of the water. "What now?" they asked.

"Look!" the lifeguard yelled. He held up a net full of the disgusting things he'd fished out of the pool.

"Oh, good!" Grouchy exclaimed. "You found our things!"

"I've had enough of you trolls!" the lifeguard yelled angrily. "You've broken all the rules, and you've made the water filthy! I'm not letting you back in until you both take a shower!"

The trolls groaned and stomped off to the locker room.

"No way am I taking a shower!" Grunty growled. He opened a locker and stashed the goodies the lifeguard had fished out inside.

"We'll pretend!" said Grouchy. "Besides, I saw something in those showers that looked like fun. Follow me!"

Chapter 4

The Grouch darted into one of
the showers and reappeared holding
something in his hand.

"Look what I found!" he cried. He
held up a squirt bottle. The liquid inside
was a disgusting green color.

"Oooh!" Grunty smiled. "That looks
just like snot!"

"I know!" Grouchy said with a giggle.
The Grunt leaned over and read the

label on the bottle: Super-Strong Shower
Gel!

"Trollrific!" Grunty's eyes lit up.

Grouchy took off the lid and squirted
the gloopy, green liquid all over himself.

He giggled. "I'm the Snotman!
And I'm gonna get you!" He dove into
another stall and grabbed a fresh bottle
of gel. Then he squirted it at Grunty!

"That's it, Grouchy!" Grunty
cried. "Now you're in for it!"
He darted off and reappeared
with his own bottle of gel.

When the trolls left the

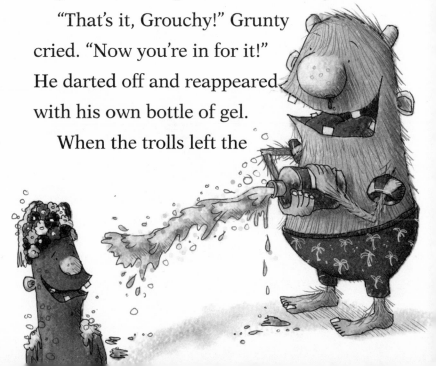

locker room a few minutes later, it looked like it had been slimed by aliens.

"That was fun!" snorted Grouchy.

"Yeah!" Grunty cried. "Now let's go back to the pool!"

The trolls kept their heads down as they squelched back out. They didn't think the lifeguard would like them being snotmen.

They hadn't gone far when Grouchy spotted a sign next to a clump of palm trees.

"Oh!" he cried. "That sounds fun! Can we go in? Please? I love bubbles!"

"Okay, Snotman!" Grunty agreed.

They followed the arrow on the sign and soon found the hot tub. There were lots of people sitting in it and enjoying the bubbles, including the father and son from earlier.

"Scoot over!" Grouchy hollered. He burst through the palm trees surrounding the hot tub and plopped down in the water.

The people in the hot tub edged away from The Grouch. Then Grunty jumped in. *BLOOP, BLOOP, BLOOP!* the hot tub filled up with giant green bubbles.

"What's going on?" yelled one of the people in the hot tub. Everyone glared at the trolls.

"Uh-oh!" Grunty said with a laugh. "It must be the Super-Strong Shower Gel!"

Everyone scrambled to their feet as

more and more bubbles erupted, spilling
over the sides of the hot tub and out
through the tropical palm trees.

Soon Grouchy was lost in a frothy fog
as more bubbles popped up.

"I think it's time for us to scram!"
Grunty said. He leaped out of the hot
tub and sprinted off to the locker room.
Grouchy chased after him like a little
swamp monster!

They grabbed their clothes from
the locker and raced to the front
door. A whistle blew loudly behind them.
TWEEET!!!

"Keep running!" cried Grunty.
"QUICK!"

Half an hour later, the trolls arrived home. They'd never run so fast or so far before. They wiped off most of the green slime and put on their clothes.

"Look at this!" cried Grunty. "My jacket fits! Must have been all that exercise!"

"Or all the stuff that washed off you in the pool!" Grouchy said.

Grunty grinned. "Right!" he cried. "Pass me the last hair cake!"

"Only if you can catch me!" Grouchy yelled. He grabbed the cake and raced upstairs.

"That's not fair!" cried Grunty,
puffing after him.

Little Monsters!

Chapter 1

SNIP! The head of a big, bright yellow sunflower tumbled to the ground.

"That's better!" Grunty said, stepping back to admire the row of tall, bare stalks. "Grouchy, how much longer will you be? I'm pooped!"

The Grouch finished watering the nettles. "There!" he said with a grin. "All done!"

"Finally!" said Grunty. "That was hard work. We deserve a nap!"

The trolls trooped inside, making sure to leave a nice muddy trail through the house behind them.

The Grunt headed straight for his big, comfy armchair with its dried-on mud patches and torn, stained fabric. He stretched and yawned and was about to flop down, when . . .

DING DONG!

"Who's that?" Grouchy grumbled.

"I don't know," The Grunt said, "but whoever it is, they're interrupting my nap!"

He stomped to the door and yanked it
open. "Get lost!" he bellowed. "Visitors
are not wel — oh, cousin Bertha!"

Grouchy raced over to the door.

There, on the *unwelcome* mat, stood a
family of trolls. The short, dumpy one
grinned at them. She was squeezed into
an orange dress and looked like a giant
pumpkin.

"Of course it's me, Grunty," she said. "Don't act like you weren't expecting us!"

Grouchy gulped. So this was Grunty's cousin, Bertha.

Next to Bertha stood a little girl troll with a twinkly tiara on her head and a tall troll as skinny as a twig. He was holding a wriggly baby who was chewing one of his ears.

Bertha nudged the tall troll's arm. "Say hello, Grimp."

"Oh, um . . . hello," Grimp mumbled.

"I'm sure you remember Pom Pom," Bertha said, pointing to the little girl. "And this is baby Grub." With that, the baby jerked around and grabbed Grunty's nose.

The Grunt sneezed, and a fountain of snot shot out of each of his nostrils.

"Goo-goo!" Grub babbled happily, clapping his tiny hands. But Pom Pom looked furious.

"My princess dress!" she shrieked, stamping her foot. "Look!" She pointed out a snotty trail sliding down her dress.

Quick as a flash, Bertha whipped out a tissue. "There there, darling," she cooed. "Grunty didn't mean to. I'll wipe it clean."

"No!" snapped Pom Pom. She tossed back her hair, folded her arms, and scowled. "Make him get it off, or I'll scream until I pop!"

Bertha quickly ushered her daughter inside and gave her a kiss on the head. "Come on, Grimp," she whispered. "Let's go before Pom Pom explodes."

Grimp quickly passed the baby to Grouchy and headed for the front door.

"See you after the wedding!" Bertha said, tossing Grunty a bag. "There are diapers and food in the baby bag, and Pom Pom brought some toys to play with. Have fun!"

"Wait!" Grunty said. "What are you talking about? What wedding? I don't know anything about a wedding!"

"I sent you a letter!" Bertha called, as she hurried down the path. "We're going to a wedding, and you're babysitting the kids."

"I didn't get a letter. The dog eats our letters!" bellowed Grunty. "BERTHA!"

But it was too late. Bertha and Grimp had disappeared, and now Grunty and Grouchy were stuck with the little monsters.

Pom Pom marched up and poked The Grunt in the stomach. "This is your snot!" she scowled.

Chapter 2

Grunty frowned and folded his arms across his chest. "No way!" he said. "I don't do cleaning!"

"You have to!" Pom Pom insisted. "I'm a little princess, and if you don't, I'll scream until I pop! And then my mom will be very angry with you!"

"Like I care!" Grunty said.

"Fine," Princess Pom Pom said with a scowl. "But I warned you. . . ."

Suddenly Grouchy shot over. The thought of Bertha being angry was scarier than cleaning.

"I'll do it!" he cried. "I'll clean off the snot! Here, Grunty, you take the baby!" He passed baby Grub over.

"Well, make sure you save all the snot!" said Grunty. "There's an empty jar on the shelf."

"I will," Grouchy said. He looked at Pom Pom and did a funny curtsy. "May I clean off the snot, um, Princess?" he asked.

"Hmmm . . ." Pom Pom said thoughtfully. "I suppose." She grabbed her toy bag and grabbed Grouchy's hand. "Let's be best friends!" she said, giggling as they headed to the kitchen.

"Okay," Grouchy said nervously. "I mean, I'd love to, Princess!"

As soon as they'd disappeared, Grunty put the baby down on the floor. Grub gazed up at him and smiled.

"You go crawl around while I take my nap," Grunty said. He walked over to his favorite chair and was about to flop down when . . .

"WAAA!" Tears were gushing from Grub's eyes, and his face had turned purple.

"What's wrong?" cried Grunty. "Okay, okay! Calm down! I'm coming!"

He dashed across the room. "Nice baby!"

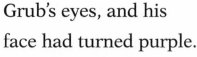

he cooed, patting Grub on the head. "There's no need for tears."

But the baby continued to cry and scream.

"Oh, I know!" said Grunty. He made his grossest were-skunk face, the one that always made Grouchy giggle. But it didn't work. The baby's eyes grew wide, and he cried even louder!

"What do you want?" asked Grunty. He knelt down beside the baby on the floor. Grub immediately stopped crying and blew a raspberry.

"Aha!" said Grunty. "You want to blow raspberries! Okay, check this out!"

With that, Grunty blew an enormous raspberry, spraying everything — including baby Grub — with spit.

Grub squealed with delight and
waved his little arms in the air. Then he
grabbed a piece of Grunty's thick, purple
hair and tugged.

And so it went. Each time Grunty
tried to escape to his chair, the baby
would start to cry. He wouldn't stop until
Grunty blew more giant raspberries.

After thirty minutes, Grunty had had

enough. "Grouchy!" he bellowed. "What are you doing in there? I need some help with this baby! Hurry!"

But Grouchy did not come running.

Grunty picked up Grub and headed to the kitchen. "How long does it take to get snot off?" he roared, bursting in.

"Ta-da!" Grouchy yelled.

Grunty's jaw dropped. Grouchy and Pom Pom both stood in the middle of the kitchen clutching paintbrushes. On the table sat a can of glittery paint.

Grunty gazed around. Absolutely everything was sparkly! The table, the chairs, the floor, and the walls all shimmered and twinkled.

"Grouchy!" Grunty snarled. "What have you done?"

"Um," Grouchy said, "well, this is our palace! I'm the prince, and Pom Pom's the princess!"

"Exactly," said Pom Pom. "Because we're best friends." Suddenly, she sniffed the air. "Ew! That baby needs its diaper changed!"

"Not it!" Grunty and Grouchy yelled at the same time.

Chapter 3

The Grouch backed away. "I can't do it," he said. "I have to finish painting my palace!"

"Not so fast!" growled Grunty. "Somebody has to change the baby's diaper!"

The Grunt thought for a minute. "I know!" he cried. "Let's do that pointy blib-blab-blob thing, and whoever lands on 'blob' has to do it."

"Do we have to?" Grouchy whined. He never won at blib-blab-blob!

Grunty ignored him. "Ready?" he asked.

Grouchy sighed. "Fine," he grumbled.

"Good!" said Grunty. "I'll do the pointing, like always."

Grunty held up a finger and started pointing back and forth between himself and Grouchy. "Blib-blab-blob. Blib-blab-blob. Blib . . . uh . . . blob!"

Grouchy groaned. Grunty's finger had landed on him again! "Why do I always lose?" he muttered.

"He cheated!" shrieked Pom Pom. "He left out a blab! You're a cheater!"

"What?" Grunty said. "I wouldn't cheat!" He quickly passed the baby to Grouchy.

"NO!" shrieked Pom Pom, glaring at The Grunt. "You cheated, so you have to change Grub's diaper! And if you don't, I'll scream until I pop!"

"That's not possible," Grunty said with a yawn.

Princess Pom Pom took a huge breath and then let out a scream so terrible that it rattled the windows and shook the walls. Even Grub started crying again.

"Stop her!" Grouchy yelled. "Before she pops!"

"She won't pop!" Grunty said. But deep down he wasn't too sure. Pom Pom's face was already turning red, and she was showing no signs of stopping.

"Okay, fine!" bellowed Grunty, rubbing his aching head. "I'll change the stupid diaper! Just stop screaming!"

Pom Pom immediately fell silent, and she smiled at The Grunt. "Grub's diaper bag is by your chair," she told him happily.

The Grunt took the baby and stomped off. Pom Pom and Grouchy trailed behind.

"What a day!" Grunty muttered. He found the diaper bag and started to undo Grub's dirty diaper.

Pom Pom climbed up on Grunty's chair so she could see better. Soon she started calling out "helpful" instructions

like, "No!" or "You're doing it wrong!" or
"Try again!"

"Go play!" Grunty snapped at her
as he struggled to fit the clean diaper
on the wriggling baby. But Pom Pom
wouldn't go.

After a lot of huffing and puffing,
Grunty finally got it right. "See," he said,

blowing a raspberry at Grub. "Nothing to it!"

Pom Pom grinned and jumped down from the chair. "Now give Grub a ride!" she commanded.

"What?" Grunty growled.

"A ride!" she said. "I want one too. You can carry me, Prince Grouch! And if you don't, I'll scream until I pop!"

Grunty sighed. He couldn't stand to hear Pom Pom start screaming again, so he picked up Grub and plopped him down on his shoulder.

"Now me!" cried

Pom Pom, jumping on Grouchy and almost flattening him. "Off we go!"

The trolls galloped around for what seemed like hours. They were exhausted.

"It must be Grub's naptime by now!" Grunty said as he collapsed into his chair.

Pom Pom giggled. "Don't be silly. It's lunchtime!" she said. "And after lunch, beautiful Princess Pom Pom, that's me, has to be rescued from a grumpy ogre!"

"Who's going be the grumpy ogre?" asked Grouchy.

"Don't look at me!" Grunty said with a scowl. "Definitely not!"

They all trooped into the kitchen. As Grunty and Grouchy tried to feed Grub a bowl of mush, Pom Pom devoured

the snack her mother had packed her:
a giant mud-cake, three packets of
cockroach chips, and a mountain of rice
pudding sandwiches.

"Save some for us!" called Grunty.
"We haven't been to the store in weeks,
and I'm starving!"

Pom Pom
grinned.
"Ooopsy!" she
cried. "Too
late! It's all
gone!"

Burping loudly, she picked up her
bag of toys and pulled out a big, wart-
covered ogre costume. "Here!" she cried,
tossing it at Grunty. "It's time for me
to be rescued, and you're the grumpy
ogre!"

Chapter 4

"What?" roared Grunty. "No way! I'm not playing!" He stared at the ogre costume. The warts were cool, but he wasn't going to tell Pom Pom that.

"You have to!" Pom Pom insisted. "Otherwise I'll scream until I pop!" She opened her mouth to scream.

"Fine, I'll try it on," Grunty said. "But I'm not playing!" He set Grub on the ground and wriggled into the costume. "Raaaghhhh!" he roared.

"Yay!" Grouchy cheered. He knew Grunty wouldn't be able to resist playing.

"That's enough," Grunty said. "I'm going to take my nap."

He thumped across the kitchen, but just as he reached the door, he heard Pom Pom say, "Prince Grouch, would you like a jelly beetle?"

"Oooh!" cried Grouchy. "We love jelly beetles, don't we, Grunty?"

Grunty spun around. "Yum!" he said. "They're delicious!"

"Too bad!" yelled Pom Pom. "Because these are only for trolls who play with me!"

Grunty gulped. "Um . . . well," he said, gazing at the bag of jelly beetles. "I suppose I could play . . . just for a bit."

"Fine!" snapped Pom Pom. "But you have to do what I say!"

With that, she pointed to the floor. "You live in under-the-table land!" she said. "All alone in a smelly cave!"

"Fine by me!" Grunty growled as he crawled under the table.

"Now cry!" said Pom Pom. "Because nobody loves you!"

Grunty gave a snotty sniff.

"Now clean up your icky cave!" Pom Pom commanded. "Go on!"

Grunty grabbed a pile of dirty socks and threw them over his shoulder. "Done!" he said. "Now give me a jelly beetle."

Pom Pom ignored him. "Now kidnap me and hide me in your cave."

Grunty rolled his eyes, but he climbed out from under the table and pushed Pom Pom into his fake cave.

"Good," said Pom Pom. "Now beg me to like you!"

Grunty gave a big yawn. "Like me," he said in a bored voice.

Princess Pom Pom stared at him. "NO!" she said. "I don't like you at all! Prince Grouch! Come and rescue me!"

"Whoopee!" Grouchy cheered, racing across the floor on his fleabaggy steed.

They skidded to a halt at Grunty's cave, and Pom Pom climbed on.

"Now we must have a ball!" she cried. "Then we'll feast on jelly beetles. Princess stories always end like that!"

"But I want my jelly beetles NOW!" roared Grunty.

"No ball, no jelly beetles!" said Pom
Pom. "And if you want to come, you'll
have to dress up nicely!" She fished
around in her toy bag and pulled out
several sparkly tutus.

"What?" Grunty yelled, shaking his
head. "No way!"

Five minutes later, they had all
gathered in the "ballroom," and the
dancing began.

"Stupid itchy skirt!" growled Grunty.
But Grouchy and Princess Pom Pom

ignored him. They seemed to be having a great time. Even Grub was laughing.

They danced on and on. Then Grunty suddenly realized something. "Hang on," he said. "Why is it so quiet?"

"Look!" whispered Grouchy, pointing at the sofa.

Baby Grub was fast asleep, and so was Pom Pom. The bag of jelly beetles sat next to her.

"Time for a feast!" whispered Grunty, grabbing the treats from the sleeping princess.

The two trolls tiptoed across the room to Grunty's chair and were both about to flop down when . . .

"We're back!" boomed Bertha, throwing open the front door. Suddenly, her jaw dropped. "My babies!" she gasped. "You got them to sleep! They never sleep! Ever!"

"It was easy-peasy!" Grouchy said.

"Well," said Bertha, "that's wonderful because we just won a vacation, and we need someone to watch the children. We'll drop them off next Monday, and you can have them for the whole week!"

Bertha and Grimp scooped up their little darlings and tiptoed toward the door.

"Hang on!" growled Grunty.

"Keep the tutus!" Bertha called, as she hurried off. "I have a feeling you're going to need them!"

Chapter 1

Clap, clap! The Grouch clapped his hands. "Grunty, can we go now?" he asked impatiently. The trolls were getting ready to go on a camping trip, and Grouchy could hardly wait.

The Grunt peered around. Their backpack was packed, Fleabag the dog was at Cousin Bertha's for the weekend, and the house looked like a dump.

"Okay!" Grunty said. "I think we're almost ready!"

He grabbed a snot-stained map and a brochure for the campsite they were staying at. "Doesn't it look great?" he asked Grouchy. "Muddyfields! What a trollrific name!"

"Yeah!" Grouchy said. "No toilets or gross showers — just a big muddy field!"

"Exactly," said Grunty, "I've got the map, so you carry the backpack."

"Fair enough!" Grouchy agreed. He picked up the backpack. "Ooof! This is heavy, Grunty. I hope it'll all fit on the bike."

"Of course it will," said Grunty as they put on their helmets. "C'mon, let's get going!"

"I get to sit in the front!" Grouchy yelled as Grunty sprinted outside. "GRUNTY! Wait for me!"

The Grouch puffed over to the front door, squeezed himself and the bulging backpack through, and slammed it shut behind him. "I want to sit in the front!" he cried. "Otherwise I won't be able to see."

The Grunt wobbled down the dusty path, but when he got to the bike, Grunty was already sitting on the front seat.

"Jump on!" Grunty yelled. "We'll switch seats halfway through."

"Fine," The Grouch said with a sigh. He climbed on the backseat. The backpack weighed a ton!

"Ready?" Grunty asked. "Off we go!" He took his fat, hairy foot off the ground and tried to push off. The bicycle wobbled from side to side, and toppled sideways into the ditch.

"Arrgh!" bellowed Grunty, as he struggled to his feet. "That backpack is way too heavy! Grouchy! What are you doing now?"

The Grouch was lying face up in the ditch, the backpack still on his back. "I'm stuck," he said. "Grunty, help!"

The Grunt reached down and pulled

The Grouch to his feet. Then Grunty grabbed the backpack and put it on his own back.

"Now, if it's okay with you, let's get going!" Grunty said. He picked up the bike and climbed back on. Grouchy climbed on behind him.

"Pedal harder!" puffed Grunty as the bike crawled along.

"I'm . . . ooo . . . ahh . . . trying . . . my
. . . best!" Grouchy panted as he pedaled
furiously.

Five minutes later, the rusty old
bicycle squeaked to a halt at an
intersection. "Are we there yet?"
Grouchy asked.

"No!" Grunty growled.
He took out the map
and licked off a
lump of earwax.
"According to
the map, the
Muddyfields
campground
is between
that squished
fly there

and this blob of ketchup here," he said. "See?"

"Is it my turn to sit in front yet?" Grouchy asked impatiently.

Grunty ignored him and stuffed the map back into his pocket. "Okay," he said. "We need to turn left, right?"

"Right," said Grouchy, sighing.

"No, LEFT!" cried Grunty.

"B-but," Grouchy stuttered, "that's what I said — right, left."

"No, not right, left!" Grunty bellowed. "Just left, right?"

Grouchy scratched his head and looked confused. But the trolls set off once again.

A few minutes later, The Grouch muttered, "I think you made a wrong turn."

"Did not!" Grunty said.

"Did so!" Grouchy argued.

"Didn't!" Grunty yelled.

"Did!"

Chapter 2

On and on the two trolls rode. They wobbled past trees . . . more trees . . . and then trees with cows underneath. But Muddyfields was still nowhere in sight.

They stopped and ate lunch and then set off once again. Every five minutes, Grouchy asked, "Are we there yet?"

When it got dark, Grunty stopped and switched on the bicycle's light.

"Can I sit at the front now?" Grouchy whined.

Grunty took out the map and peered at it. They were very lost.

"Are we lost?" Grouchy asked.

"No!" Grunty snapped. "Of course not!" He looked around desperately. Suddenly he spotted something. What a stroke of luck! There, in a field just over the hedge, was a cluster of tents.

"Look!" cried Grunty. "It's Muddyfields!" He jumped off the bike and raced toward the hedge.

"I told you we weren't lost!" he yelled back to Grouchy. "Well, what are you waiting for? Come on!"

The Grunt marched around the hedge and in through a gate, leaving Grouchy to push the bike by himself. Grouchy rang its bell excitedly.

They passed a farmhouse. *Ding-ding!* rang Grouchy. The front door burst open. *Ding —*

"Stop ringing that bell!" a short, plump man yelled at them. He was wearing pajamas tucked into his boots and holding a big lantern. "It's the middle of the night! You'll wake the campers!"

"Sorry!" Grouchy said. "Mr., uh . . ."

"Glum!" the man replied. He looked the trolls up and down. "Now then, who are you?"

"We're trolls," said Grunty. "And we've come to Muddyfields for our vacation!"

"So can we please put up our tent?" The Grouch asked.

Mr. Glum scowled at them. "But Muddyfields is miles away!" he said. "This is Sunnydales!"

"Oh, no," Grouchy groaned wearily.

"Oh, well," said Grunty. "I'm sure this campsite is just as good as Muddyfields!"

"As good as? It's a hundred times better!" Mr. Glum snapped. "I suppose you can stay the night."

He marched the trolls over to an empty section of the field. "You can set up your tent here. But there will be no shouting, no partying, and no littering," he told them. "And absolutely no bell ringing!"

With that, Mr. Glum stomped away.

"Well," whispered Grunty, "let's put up the tent!"

The trolls got to work, but putting up their tent in the dark was much more difficult than they'd thought. And the more they tried, the grumpier (and noisier) they became.

"Too flat . . ." moaned Grunty.

"Too lumpy . . ." groaned Grouchy.

"Watch out!" Grunty yelled.

"Now I'm stuck!" Grouchy hollered.

Finally Grunty stamped his foot. "I GIVE UP!" he yelled.

"Be quiet!" someone yelled from a nearby tent.

"Yeah!" came a voice from another.

"Mom!" wailed a boy in the tent next to theirs. "What's that noise? It sounds like monsters!"

A very long time later, their tent was finally up. "Now, let's get some sleep!" growled Grunty, crawling inside.

Grouchy scrambled in behind him and flopped down. It had been a very long day. He turned over and tried to get comfy, but it was no good. His side of the tent was way too bumpy.

"Grunty," he called, "can we switch sides?"

"Nope!" The Grunt said.

"But you'll love this side!" Grouchy argued. "It's trollrific over here!"

"I like it where I am. Now go to sleep!" Grunty closed his eyes.

"I'm cold," Grouchy grumbled. "Grunty!" He nudged him, but Grunty let out a loud, snotty snore.

GRUNTY... WILL YOU TELL ME A STORY?

Chapter 3

Next morning, Grouchy woke up bright and early. "Grunty!" he hollered. "Wake up!"

He poked The Grunt, who woke up with a start. "What's going on?" he yelled.

"It's time to get up!" cried Grouchy. "Let's go and explore! We couldn't see a thing when we got here last night! There might even be a swamp!"

The Grouch scrabbled over to the tent door, undid the ties, and popped his small, green head outside.

"Oh, no!" he gasped. "Grunty, look!"

The Grunt crawled over, stuck his head out of the tent, and gazed around the campsite.

"YUCK!" he cried.

Sunnydales was revolting. There were flowerbeds. There were fountains. There were rows of bright, clean tents. Freshly washed clothes hung on neat little washing lines. Families cooked on big, fancy barbeques. They could even see showers and . . . toilets!

The trolls shuddered. "This is not how camping is supposed to be!" Grouchy said.

"That's it!" cried Grunty. "Take down the tent! We're not staying here!"

"Can't we at least have breakfast first?" Grouchy asked. "I'm starving!"

They crawled outside and sat on the grass. The delicious smell of sausage and bacon wafted through the air.

"Well," said Grunty, "how about we light a campfire and cook up some grub before we go?"

"Okay!" said Grouchy. "I'll go collect some firewood."

Five minutes later he was back, and the trolls lit a roaring fire. They'd just started cooking when . . .

"Hey!" Mr. Glum yelled, shaking his fist. "Fires are not allowed! No shouting, no partying, no littering, no ringing bells, and NO FIRES!"

He threw a bucket of water over the flames and shook his head. "I knew you two would be trouble. This is your last chance! Do you hear me?"

"Now look what you did!" Grunty said. Mr. Glum muttered something under his breath and marched away.

"Hey!" Grouchy exclaimed. "I've got an idea." He grabbed a fishing pole from one of the gnomes that decorated the campground. "He didn't say we couldn't go fishing, did he?"

"Huh?" Grunty looked puzzled. "What do you mean?"

"Come on!" Grouchy said. "Let's go catch some breakfast!"

The trolls tiptoed to a nearby tent and hid behind it. A man stood out front cooking at a barbecue.

The trolls waited with their fishing poles until he stepped back inside the tent.

"Okay," Grouchy whispered excitedly. "Here goes!"

He swung the fishing rod and hooked

a giant sausage off the
barbeque.

"Wow!" Grunty said. "Now
how about some bacon?"

After a big breakfast, the trolls
packed up their tent. They were just
about to climb back on their bike when
suddenly . . .

"Wait!" cried Grouchy. "What's that
noise? It sounds like laughter."

"It's coming from behind that bush,"
whispered Grunty. "Let's go and see."

Chapter 4

The trolls peered over the bush and gasped with excitement at what they saw.

"Wow!" cried Grouchy. "Not quite a swamp, but it's almost as good."

"It sure is!" Grunty agreed.

A stone's throw away was a lake dotted with rowboats. Most were filled with happy families, but one small boat was empty.

"Let's play Pirate Rats!" Grunty suggested.

"Trollrific idea!" Grouchy replied. Pirate Rats was one of their favorite games. "I'll be Captain Blackwhiskers!"

"No, I get to be Captain Blackwhiskers!" growled Grunty.

They darted down to the water's edge

and jumped into the boat. Everyone else glanced across nervously.

"Yo-ho! I'm a pirate!" yelled Grunty, grabbing the oars. He started rowing like crazy, sending giant ripples through the water.

"You're a terrible captain!" The Grouch yelled as the little boat spun in circles. "You can't even row straight!"

"That's enough from you!" roared Grunty. "Now you'll have to walk the plank!"

He raised an oar into the air and started poking Grouchy. Everyone else shook their heads and scowled at the trolls.

"Oh, no!" Grunty yelled suddenly. His fingers slipped, and the oar fell into the water.

"Serves you right!" Grouchy said.

Grunty leaned over the side of the boat and reached out his hand to grab the oar that was floating in the water. The boat wobbled dangerously.

"Keep still!" yelled The Grouch. "Do you want to knock us both in the water? We'll get clean!"

But it was too late. The boat wobbled and tipped over. The Grunt and The Grouch both fell overboard and into the water.

"Arrgh!" Grouchy spluttered. "That's it! I'm going home!"

Kicking his legs wildly, The Grouch

started swimming for shore. But he hadn't gone far when something brown and drippy hit him in the back of the head. He whipped around and saw Grunty standing up in the lake.

"It's shallow!" The Grunt yelled. "And really muddy on the bottom!"

"Oh, boy!" Grouchy yelled, cheering up immediately. "Trollrific!"

He stood up. "Whoops!" he cried, as the water came up to his chin. He dove under, scooped up some mud, and flung it at The Grunt.

Smack! The mud hit Grunty right in the middle of his big purple nose.

"Mud fight!" The Grunt yelled. "Yippee!"

Ten minutes later, the Pirate Rats surveyed their kingdom. This was more like it. One gigantic mud bath!

"Maybe we should stay here after all," The Grunt said.

"Or maybe not . . ." whispered Grouchy. "Look behind you!"

The Grunt turned around. A mob of furious, mud-splattered people were rowing straight toward them.

"Uh-oh!" Grunty muttered. "To the bicycle! Quick!"

The trolls waded quickly out of the murky water and squelched up the hill to the campground.

"Look!" cried Grouchy, as they shot

around the bush. The people from the
lake were hot on their heels.

"Bike!" panted Grunty. "Jump on!"

The trolls hopped on their bike
and squeaked off at breakneck speed.

"Hey!" yelled Mr. Glum, joining
in the chase. "Come back and clean up
my campground!"

But the trolls were already halfway
down the lane.

Three hours later, Grunty stopped the
bike. "Okay, Grouchy," he puffed. "You
can sit in the front now!"

"Finally!" The Grouch climbed down off his seat. "Wait a minute!" he cried. "Grunty, we're home!"

"Oh, yeah!" The Grunt said with a laugh. "I guess we are."

"Hooray!" the trolls cried, diving into their swampy garden. And for once, they agreed . . . there was no place quite like home.

Tracey Corderoy

was born and grew up in South Wales before moving to Bath, England to become a teacher. Tracey has always been passionate about writing for children and convinced that language, expressed through wonderful literature, is the key to stimulating learning and imagination. She currently lives in an ancient cottage with her husband, two daughters, and their many animals.

Lee Wildish

lives in Lancashire, England and has been drawing since a very young age. He loves illustrating children's books and thinks there's nothing better than seeing people laughing at a book he's illustrated.

READ MORE ABOUT **THE GRUNT AND THE GROUCH** AT capstonekids.com/characters/grunt-grouch